ARTHUR
AND THE
ICE RINK

Johanne Mercier
Daniel Hahn
Clare Elsom

PHOE

More stories
with Arthur

1. Arthur and the Mystery of the Egg

2. Arthur and the Earthworms

3. Arthur and the Yeti

4. Arthur and the Guard Dog

5. Arthur and the Witch

6. Arthur and the Ice Rink

CONTENTS

For little Romy

JM

For Julia

DH

For Kieran

CE

Chapter 1
The Famous Gold Medal

I'm Arthur and I'm seven, and in the summer holidays I always have a great time at my grandparents' house in the country. But when it's winter, I sometimes get a bit bored. Last Friday, I didn't really want to spend the weekend at Picket Lake. Fortunately, my mum had a brilliant idea.

"Oh, you've brought your ice skates!" said Grandma, as she opened my bags.

"Can I go skating now?"

She gave my grandfather a look.

I realised there was a little problem.

"We'll find a solution, Arthur," said Grandad.

The problem was that there wasn't an ice rink at my grandparents' house. And their neighbours didn't have one either. And neither did Cousin Eugene.

I was so disappointed.

"Have you ever been ice skating, Grandad?"

"Who, me? I won the gold medal for the Great Crossing of Picket Lake, young Arthur."

I'd never heard of the Great Crossing of Picket Lake, ever, in my whole life.

"Haven't you seen my gold medal?" asked my grandfather, amazed.

He went up to the attic and I followed him.

Grandad emptied out a big box, filled with things he hadn't seen for ages. He found his old hat from cricket with holes in it, a signed cricket bat, some very yellowy newspapers and a brilliant collection of matchboxes.

But he didn't find his medal.

His good mood had disappeared, too.

"Well, well," said Grandma when we came back down from the attic. "I'm going to call Eugene."

"You think Eugene has Grandad's medal?"

"No, Arthur, but I'm sure Eugene has one or two photos of the Great Crossing."

A few minutes later, Eugene arrived, carrying seven big photo albums.

Chapter 2

Eugene's big Plan

Grandad really was very pleased to see the hundreds of photos of the Great Crossing again. I looked at them all with him.

"Was it a real gold medal?" I asked.

"Solid gold, my boy!"

Grandma gave me a wink, like she always did when Grandad was exaggerating.

"You skated across the whole lake?"

"I was the champion!"

This time, Grandma agreed, but she

added that their neighbour, Mrs Potter, had been pretty quick, too. She had come second.

"Why aren't we allowed to skate on the lake anymore?"

They both shrugged. They didn't know why.

"I've got an idea!" Eugene cried, suddenly. "An inspired idea! A magnificent idea!"

"Are we going to make a giant skating rink on the lake?"

"Better than that, Arthur. I'm going to organise another Great Crossing. Just like we used to have!"

"Oh, good grief," growled Grandad.

"You have nothing to be afraid of, Uncle Geoffrey. I'll take care of everything."

"That's just what I'm afraid of."

Then Eugene looked at the three of us, and asked, "You will help me, won't you?"

"Eugene, didn't you just say *you* would

take care of everything?"

"Absolutely, Uncle Geoffrey! And right now, I'm taking care of finding just the right people to do the work!"

Grandma promised to help out. I did, too. Finally, Grandad told Eugene he could count on him.

Chapter 3
The Invitations

Grandad and I were in charge of the invitations. We started by visiting my grandparents' neighbour, Mrs Potter. When my grandfather told her about the plans for the Great Crossing of Picket Lake, she smiled. And since Mrs Potter doesn't smile very often, I thought this was a good start.

"The Great Crossing of Picket Lake?"

"That's right, Alison."

"On ice skates?"

"Of course."

"Like twenty years ago?"

"Um… yes..."

"With medals being handed out?"

"Obviously!"

"In that case... no!"

Mrs Potter shut the door and my grandfather was sure she was never going to change her mind. Then we visited lots of other neighbours to tell them about Eugene's plan. We saw

the Harveys, the Hudsons, and all the others who lived around the lake. But nobody had time to take part in the Great Crossing.

Everyone wished us good luck all the same.

We came back home, quite sad.

"Well?" asked Cousin Eugene, who was waiting for us, sitting quietly, watching television. "Did you sign up a lot of people to take part in the competition? Twenty? Thirty? Fifty? A hundred?"

"Zero," I said.

"No one?" said Eugene, very disappointed.

"Not a mouse," muttered Grandad.

But since other people had started to use the lake as an ice rink anyway, I asked, "Can I go skating?"

"Very soon, Arthur," replied Eugene. "First, we need to make a plan, team!"

Chapter 4
The brilliant Solution

When nobody accepts an invitation, it's because you've forgotten to mention that there will be little snacks for them to eat," said Grandma.

"Most certainly, Aunt Margaret," replied Cousin Eugene.

I agreed, because I love little snacks.

"We'll make a delicious barbecue," suggested Eugene, "with pork chops!"

But Grandad told him the barbecue idea was overdoing it a bit.

"Maybe people will come anyway, just for the skating," I said.

"Just for the skating?" Eugene repeated.

"Without any medals?" grumbled Grandad. "It's a lot less fun without medals."

"Bah! In any case, you only end up losing those old medals of yours," said Grandma.

"Arthur's right!" exclaimed Eugene. "We'll open a simple little ice rink, without any song and dance, without any bells or whistles!"

"You'll still need some music," said Grandma. "It's very, very important to have music when you ice-skate."

"Indeed, Aunt Margaret. Skaters often use waltzes to keep time."

"We'll need to set up some benches, too," added Grandad. "For people who want a rest."

"Or for the people eating pork chops."

"Just forget about your pork chops, Eugene!"

"We are going to have pork chops, Uncle Geoffrey."

"Well, then we are going to have medals!"

"Pork chops are more important!"

"Medals!"

"Pork chops!"

"Medals!"

"What babies you are," sighed Grandma. "So long as there's music…"

I asked if I could go skating even if there weren't any benches, music or pork chops. But no one answered because they were all too busy.

Later, Grandad went out to borrow the benches from Mrs Potter.

"The big benches from my garden?"

"Yes, Alison."

"The ones in the snow?"

"Of course."

"Well, Geoffrey Franklin, just don't expect me to help with the shovelling."

"Arthur will give me a hand," said Grandad, putting his arm around my shoulders.

Mrs Potter rolled her eyes. She sighed. She grumbled. But she agreed.

It wasn't easy to get the benches out. It was cold, but we were working so hard we didn't even notice. We put the two benches

alongside the ice rink and went back home.

When I asked Grandma if I could have a hot chocolate to warm up, Eugene started yelling.

"HOT CHOCOLATE!
HOT CHOCOLATE!
WHAT WAS I THINKING?

An ice rink isn't an ice rink without hot chocolate!"

Then Grandad had to build a shelter with a table underneath it, and on that table he

put a thermos flask, and in that thermos flask… hot chocolate.

"You can go ice skating now, young Arthur," Grandad announced, finally. "Everything is ready!"

But Grandma reminded us that it was actually dinner time.

I couldn't wait for it to be the next morning.

Chapter 5
Sunday already

During the night, heaps of snow fell everywhere. Cousin Eugene arrived at my grandparents' house very early. He announced that we would have to shovel the snow off everything.

We had to shovel to find the ice rink.

And we had to shovel to find the table for the hot chocolate.

And the benches.

And everything else.

We even had to shovel to find the other

shovel that I'd left by the side of the lake.

Grandad got his loudspeakers, which he put out on the porch, and Grandma turned on some music. She told me they were waltzes. And waltzes help you skate… and also shovel.

Mrs Potter was at the window, watching us through her binoculars. Grandad waved for her to join us, but she pulled down her blind.

"Why does Mrs Potter get angry when we talk about the Great Crossing?" I asked.

"Because she's a sore loser," replied Grandad, with a chuckle.

While we worked, Eugene sat on a bench and kept reading over his list of things that needed to be done.

"Why don't you come and help us instead?" shouted Grandma.

"I'm just polishing off the final arrangements for the event, Aunt Margaret."

"Surely you can polish while you're shovelling!" growled Grandad.

But Eugene didn't move.

When all the work was finished, he got up and said:

"My friends, I can tell you that we are now officially ready to open the Picket Lake Ice Rink."

"And I can tell you that you won't do anything of the sort!" added a stern voice from behind Eugene.

It was a little round man, who was wearing glasses that were also round.

He wasn't smiling.

And he didn't look like he wanted to smile either.

Chapter 6
The Guest of Honour

The round man was the mayor. He took a bit of paper out of his pocket, unfolded it and read: "Municipal regulation 723, paragraph 29, forbidding the organisation of a competitive event resembling the Great Crossing of Picket Lake."

He showed the piece of paper to Eugene, who gave it to Grandad, who didn't even look at it.

Grandma rushed over towards the visitor. "Mr Mayor…"

He took three steps back.

"Do you know how to skate?"

He stepped back even further.

"Do you like to skate?"

"When I was little, I rather…"

"Do you like pork chops?"

"When they're done in a lovely sweet sauce I'd never say no."

"You are our guest of honour!"

"Me?"

The mayor slipped the piece of paper with the regulations back into his pocket. At that moment, Mrs Potter came out of her house. She was wearing a funny overcoat with a round thing made from pink fur to keep her hands warm.

"So, Geoffrey Franklin, you've heard about the regulation then?" she said, smiling something that wasn't a real smile.

"There isn't going to be a Great Crossing

of the lake, Alison," announced Grandma.

"Not at all. This is just the opening of our ice rink," explained Eugene.

"And there are going to be pork chops!" added the mayor.

"No medals, but pork chops?" repeated Mrs Potter. "Now I've heard it all!"

And Grandad whispered in my ear: "Quick, go get your skates on, Arthur!"

But as I was running towards the house, I heard a voice calling: "Arthuuuuuuur!"

It was my mum.

My weekend in the country was already over!

When I went to say goodbye to everyone, Grandma was serving Mrs Potter some hot chocolate; Grandad was trying to light the barbecue in the snow; Cousin Eugene was taking hundreds of photos of Grandad with the barbecue; and the mayor was

holding his little plate, waiting for the pork chops.

All five of them really were having a great time.

And that afternoon, when Grandad put on the old winter coat he hadn't worn in years, guess what he found in the pocket?

ARTHUR

Johanne Mercier

It all started when this lady called Johanne thought about me in her head. Grandma said Johanne had written fifty-eight stories for children, and that one of her stories was made into a film. Grandma also said Johanne understands children because she used to be a teacher. But now she writes all day.

I think it must be really fun to write stories all day. When I grow up, I want to write stories like Johanne Mercier, and I also want to be a pilot. Grandad says there's nothing to stop me doing both, but I think that writing stories and flying a plane at the same time is not a good idea.

Daniel Hahn

Daniel Hahn translated the stories. He took my French words, and wrote them in English. He said it was quite a difficult job, but Cousin Eugene said he could have done it much better, only he was busy that day. So we got Daniel to do it, as he's translated loads and loads of books before. He also said he wrote the words for a book called *Happiness is a Watermelon on your Head*, but everyone else said that book was just plain silly.

Daniel is almost as clever as Cousin Eugene and he lives in England, in a house by the sea, with a lot of books.

Clare Elsom

I was so happy when we met Clare Elsom. She got out her pencils and pens and scribbled until the scribbles looked just like me! Grandma and Grandad said the resemblance was uncanny.

Clare has so many pencils and pens – at least twenty of them – and she spends all day drawing in lots of different books. I'm not sure that you are allowed to draw in books, but she seems to get away with it.

I like Clare because she likes egg on toast and exploring new places, and drawing me. But I think she wants my pet duck, so I will have to keep an eye on her.

More escapades with
Arthur coming soon

What would you like Arthur to do next?
Send us your ideas for Arthur's adventures:
arthur@phoenixyardbooks.com

Also available

ARTHUR

AND THE WITCH

JOHANNE MERCIER

Arthur and the Ice Rink
ISBN: 978-1-907912-21-4

First published in French in 2012 under the title *Arthur et la patinoire géante*
by Dominique et compagnie, a division of Les Editions Heritage, Saint-Lambert,
Canada. This edition published in the UK by Phoenix Yard Books Ltd, 2013.

Phoenix Yard Books
Phoenix Yard
65 King's Cross Road
London
WC1X 9LW
www.phoenixyardbooks.com

Text copyright © Johanne Mercier, 2012
English translation copyright © Daniel Hahn, 2013
Illustrations copyright © Clare Elsom, 2013

1 3 5 7 9 10 8 6 4 2
A CIP catalogue record for this book is available from the British Library
Printed in China